Big Momma
Makes the
World

For Amy with love ✦ P. R.

To Hattie ✦ H. O.

First U.S. edition 2003

Library of Congress Cataloging-in-Publication Data
Root, Phyllis.
Big Momma makes the world / Phyllis Root & Helen Oxenbury. —1st U.S. ed.
p.   cm.
Summary: Big Momma, with a baby on her hip and laundry piling up,
makes the world and everything in it and, at the end of the sixth day,
tells the people she has made that they must take care of her creation.
ISBN 0-7636-1132-8
[1. Creation—Fiction.] I. Oxenbury, Helen, ill. II. Title.
PZ7.R6784 Bi 2002
E—dc21   2002017498

10 9 8 7 6 5 4 3 2 1

Printed in Italy

This book was typeset in StonePrint and Aquinas.
The illustrations were done in acrylic.

Candlewick Press
2067 Massachusetts Avenue
Cambridge, Massachusetts 02140

visit us at www.candlewick.com

BIG MOMMA MAKES THE WORLD

written by Phyllis Root

illustrated by Helen Oxenbury

CANDLEWICK PRESS
CAMBRIDGE, MASSACHUSETTS

When Big Momma made the world,
she didn't mess around.

There was water, water everywhere,
and Big Momma saw what needed
to be done all right.
So she rolled up her sleeves and went to it.
Wasn't easy, either, with that little baby
sitting on her hip.
Didn't stop Big Momma, though.
Not for a minute.

"Light," said Big Momma.
And you better believe there was light.

"Dark," said Big Momma,
and there was the dark,
just as big as the light.

"You two got work to do,"
Big Momma said.
"Don't you be fooling around none."

Then she looked at the light

and she looked at the dark,

and she looked at that little baby

looking at the light and the dark,

smiling and cooing,

and Big Momma said,

"That's good. That's real good."

That's how the first day went by.

Next day Big Momma looked around.
   "Can't tell my up from my down,"
   said Big Momma.
"Better have some sky here."
   And there it was,
      one big sky wrapping over everything,
      soft and blue as a baby's blanket.
   Wasn't much else yet
      but water and light and dark and sky,
      all doing what Big Momma
      wanted them to do,
      and Big Momma, she was pleased all right.
"That's good," she said. "That's real good."

   That's how the second day went by.

Next day Big Momma
    looked around some more and she said,
    "Got me some light,
    got me some dark,
    but I still can't tell what time of day it is.
How am I gonna know when it's morning?
Evening?
Time to put the baby down for a nap?"
Big Momma, she wanted to know all right,
    and anything Big Momma wants,
    Big Momma gets. That's just how it goes.

"Sun," said Big Momma,
    "you take care of this day business for me."

"Moon," said Big Momma,
   "you take care of the night."

Big Momma made the stars, too,
   just in case old moon overslept sometime.
Big Momma looked at the sun and the moon
   and the stars filling up her sky,
   just in time for the little baby's nap,
   and Big Momma nodded,
   and she smiled,
   and she said,
   "That's good. That's real good."

That's how the third day went by.

Next morning Big Momma got up
with the sun, and she said,
"I need a place to put my feet down
when they need putting down."
She knew there'd be some foot-putting-down
when that baby of hers got to growing more.
"Earth," said Big Momma, "get over here."
And it did.
All one big ball of mud it was,
nothing much to look at.
Baby liked it all right just the way it was,
but Big Momma wasn't finished yet.

"Need some grass to wriggle my toes in,"
        said Big Momma.
    "Some big old shade trees for hanging a hammock.
    Papayas and oranges and boysenberries for eating on."
    That's how it was then,
        just like Big Momma said,
        little baby sucking on a mango,
        and grass and trees and fruit
        all over the place,
        like somebody tipped over a fruit stand.
    Big Momma, she looked at all that earth, and she said,
        "That's good. That's real good."

    That's how the fourth day went by.

Lots of folks would be plenty pleased,
    but Big Momma, she doesn't quit
    a job till it's done and done right.
Big Momma looked at
    all that water and earth
    and trees and sky and sun
    and moon and stars, and she said,
    "Awful quiet down there.
Better have some whales,
    better have some birds,
    better have some fish."

That's exactly what happened all right.
   Pretty soon there were more whales and
      catfish and mockingbirds and crows
      than a little baby could shake a stick at,
      which a little baby could do
      if a little baby wanted to,
      since Big Momma had already made
      all those trees full of sticks.
   Big Momma looked at all that action, and she said,
      "That's good. That's real good."

   That's how the fifth day went by.

Big Momma was about ready to be done with it all.
Making a world was a lot of work,
what with the laundry piling up
and the dishes needing doing.
She figured she better finish things off in one big bang.
"I need me some creepers and crawlers,"
said Big Momma.
"Some runners and jumpers.
Some diggers and divers.
Everybody else wants to get created,
this here's your chance."
Hedgehogs and night crawlers, raccoons
and garter snakes, rabbits and polar bears,
that's how Big Momma made them all.

One Big Bang!

But Big Momma still wasn't done. Oh, no.

"I'm lonely," said Big Momma.
"Who's gonna sit on the front porch
        and swap stories with me?
Not these creepers and crawlers.
Not these diggers and divers.
They're good all right,
        but not one of them can tell a story
        worth a plug nickel.
And all this little baby can say so far
        is goo-goo-ga-ga.
I need some folks to keep me company."

Big Momma,
>   she scooped up some of that leftover mud,
>
>   and she pushed, and she pulled,
>
>   and she poked, and she pried,
>
>   and the next thing you know,
>
>   there were folks everywhere.

Big folks and little folks.

Fat folks and thin folks.

All kinds of shades of folks.

And every one of those folks
>   had a story to swap with Big Momma.

"That's good," said Big Momma.
>   "That's real good."

That's how the sixth day went by,
    with Big Momma and all those folks
    sitting on the porch and gabbing
    while the sun went down.

Big Momma was ready for a rest all right,
  ready to bundle up with that little baby of hers
  in that big blue blanket of the sky.

But Big Momma had one more thing to do.
She lined up all those folks and said,
  "This is a real nice world we got here,
  and you all better take some good care of it.
I'm taking a day off to rest now,
  but I'll be keeping an eye on you."

That's what Big Momma said all right.
And you better believe she meant it.

Every once in a while,

    when she's burping the baby

    or making cookies

    or rocking that little baby to sleep,

Big Momma looks down and says,

    "Better straighten up down there."

And every so often Big Momma looks down
on this nice little world
she made and she nods and
she smiles, and she says,

"That's good. That's real good."